Laugh-Out-Loud
Awesome
Jokes for Kids

LAUGH
-Out-
LOUD
AWESOME
JOKES
for KIDS

ROB ELLIOTT

HARPER
An Imprint of HarperCollins Publishers

Laugh-Out-Loud Awesome Jokes for Kids

Copyright © 2017 by Robert Elliott Teigen

All rights reserved. Printed in the United States of America.

For information address HarperCollins Children's Books, a division of HarperCollins Publishers, 195 Broadway, New York, NY 10007.

www.harpercollinschildrens.com

Library of Congress Control Number: 2016957947

ISBN 978-0-06-249795-6

Typography by Gearbox

17 18 19 20 21   PC/BRR   10 9

❖

First Edition

To my wife, Joanna. Everyone needs someone who helps them through the good days and bad—she's my awesome!

Q: Why can't you trust artists?

A: They're sketchy.

Q: Why did the baseball coach go to the bakery?

A: He needed a batter.

Q: What is a tree's favorite drink?

A: Root beer.

Q: Where do you take a bad rainbow?

A: To prism.

Q: What kind of monster never irons its clothes?

A: A wash-and-wear-wolf.

- -

Q: What do you call someone who grabs your cat and runs?

A: A purr snatcher.

Q: How do you get a bargain on a cruise vacation?

A: Look for a clearance sail.

Knock, knock.

Who's there?

To.

To who?

Don't you mean "to whom"?

Q: What did the buck say to the doe?

A: "I'm fawned of you, my deer."

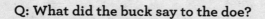

- -

Knock, knock.

Who's there?

Ache.

Ache who?

Bless you!

Bob: Did you hear about the farmer who wrote a joke book?

Bill: No, is it any good?

Bob: The jokes are pretty corny!

Knock, knock.

Who's there?

Hector.

Hector who?

When the Hector you going to open the door?

- -

Emma: Can February March?

Leah: No, but April May!

Q: What do you call a nose with no body?

A: Nobody knows!

Q: Which has more courage, a rock or a tree?

A: A rock, because it's boulder!

Josh: Do you think change is hard?

Joe: I sure do! Have you ever tried to bend

a quarter?

Dave: Did you like my joke about the fish?

Adam: Not really.

Dave: Well, if you can think of a better fish joke, let minnow!

Isaiah: How smart are you, Mason?

Mason: I'm so bright my mom calls me "sun"!

Stanley: What happened when you found out your toaster wasn't waterproof?

Dudley: I was shocked!

Q: Why did the banana put on sunscreen?

A: It was starting to peel.

Q: Why did the Starburst go to school?

A: He wanted to be a Smartie!

- -

Patient: Doctor, I think I'm turning into a piano.

Doctor: Well, that's just grand!

Q: Where do you learn to saw wood?

A: In a boarding school.

Q: What is a soda's favorite subject in school?

A: Fizz-ics!

Q: Why don't grapes snore when

  they're sleeping?

A: They don't want to wake the rest of the bunch.

Q: What's a cow's favorite painting?

A: The *Moo-na Lisa*.

Knock, knock.

Who's there?

Rita.

Rita who?

Rita good book lately?

Knock, knock.

Who's there?

Ears.

Ears who?

Ears looking at you, kid!

- -

Q: What is a dentist's favorite time of day?

A: Tooth-thirty.

Q: What happens to toilet paper with good grades?

A: It goes on the honor roll!

Q: Which tree is always at the doctor's office?

A: A sick-amore tree!

Q: Why did the boy eat his homework?

A: Because the teacher said it was a piece of cake.

Q: What do you get when you throw noodles in a Jacuzzi?

A: Spaghetti.

Q: Why did the hog have a stomachache?

A: He pigged out at dinner.

Q: Why did the stereo blow up?

A: It was radioactive!

Q: How do you know when a bucket feels sick?

A: It looks a little pail.

Q: What plays music in your hair?

A: A headband!

- -

Q: What kind of bird is with you at every meal?

A: A swallow.

Q: What goes ho-ho-ho, scratch-scratch-scratch?

A: Santa Claws!

Q: What are a hyena's favorite cookies?

A: Snickerdoodles!

Q: Why couldn't the beaver work on his computer?

A: He forgot to log in.

Q: What do you call a dog wearing earplugs?

A: It doesn't matter—it can't hear you anyway!

Q: How much did Santa's sleigh cost?

A: Nothing, it was on the house!

Q: What is a skeleton's favorite instrument?

A: A trombone.

Jenny: I should give my pig a bubble bath.

Johnny: That's hogwash!

Q: Why did the clock go back four seconds?

A: It was really hungry!

Q: Why did the clam go to the gym?

A: To work out its mussels.

- -

Q: Why did the doctor send the book to the hospital?

A: It had to remove its appendix.

Jim: I need someone to help me build an ark.

Bob: I think I Noah guy!

Q: What do you call a fake noodle?

A: An im-pasta.

Q: What has four legs but can't walk?

A: A chair.

Q: What kind of shoes does a ninja wear?

A: Sneakers.

Q: Why don't frogs die from laryngitis?

A: Because they can't croak!

Q: Why was the eye doctor sent home from the party?

A: He was making a spectacle of himself.

-- -- -- -- -- -- -- -- -- -- -- -- -- -- -- -- --

Q: What kind of underwear does a lawyer wear?

A: Briefs.

Q: When does a hot dog get in trouble?

A: When it's being a brat.

Jimmy: That soda just hit me on the head!

Bobby: Oh no, are you OK?!

Jimmy: Yeah, luckily it was a soft drink.

Emma: Did you like your book about gravity?

Leah: Yes, I couldn't put it down!

Q: Why did the boy stop using his pencil?

A: It was pointless.

Q: Why did the ruler fail in school?

A: It didn't measure up.

Q: Why did the wood fall asleep?

A: It was board.

Q: Why did the bee need allergy medicine?

A: It had hives.

Q: What do you get when you cross a judge and a skunk?

A: Odor in the court!

- -

Q: Why was the peanut mad at the pretzel?

A: It was in-salt-ing him.

Q: What kind of potato do you see on the news?

A: A commen-tater.

Q: Why did the pig get out of bed?

A: It was time to rise and swine!

Q: What is E. T. short for?

A: Because his legs are so little!

Q: What is the most negative month of the year?

A: November!

Q: How does a deer carry its lunch?

A: In a bucket!

- -

Q: Why did the bee go to the barber?

A: He wanted a buzz cut.

Q: How do you make your shoe stay quiet?

A: Put a sock in it!

Q: What's a plumber's favorite instrument?

A: A pipe organ.

Q: Why shouldn't you have plastic surgery?

A: Because it's rude to pick your nose.

Q: Why did the baker have a rash?

A: Because he was making bread from scratch!

- -

Q: How did the celery get rich?

A: It invested in the stalk market.

Q: What do you get when you throw a rooster in the bathroom?

A: A cock-a-doodle-loo!

Q: What do you call a can of Jell-O?

A: Gelatin.

Q: Who's in charge of the tissue company?

A: The handkerchief.

- -

Q: How do owls like their rabbits for breakfast?

A: Bunny-side up!

Q: What do bunny rabbits eat in the summer?

A: Hop-sickles.

Q: Why do cannibals like dentists the best?

A: They're the most filling!

- -

Q: Why wouldn't the dentist tell the patient about his cavities?

A: He didn't want to hurt his fillings!

Q: Why did the egg get kicked out of the comedy club?

A: He was telling bad yokes.

Q: Why did Humpty Dumpty get sent to the principal's office?

A: Because he was a rotten egg!

Q: Why was the egg afraid to meet new people?

A: He was a little chicken.

- -

Q: What do you get when you wear a watch for a belt?

A: A waist of time!

Q: Why did the lumberjack chop down the wrong tree?

A: It was an axe-ident.

Q: Why did the chicken go to the gym?

A: It needed more eggs-ercise!

Q: Why did the rabbit go to the salon?

A: She was having a bad hare day.

- -

Preston: Why did all the chickens disappear?

Winston: I don't have any eggs-planation!

Q: Who brings Easter eggs to all the sea creatures?

A: The oyster bunny.

Q: What do you get when you cross a dog and a crab?

A: A Doberman pincher.

Q: Why did the meteor do well in school?

A: It was the teacher's star pupil.

Q: What do you call a friendly scoop of frozen yogurt?

A: Nice cream!

Q: What do you call a mad biscuit?

A: A hot cross bun!

Q: Why did the baker study hard in school?

A: So he could make the honor roll!

Q: Why did the carpenter quit using his drill?

A: Because it was always boring.

Q: Why did the carpenter become a comedian?

A: He had a really funny drill bit.

Q: When doesn't a lamb spend any money?

A: When it's a sheep-skate!

Q: How does a blacksmith send a letter?

A: In an anvil-ope.

Q: What kind of room has no doors or windows?

A: A mushroom.

Q: What kind of animal will fix your leaky pipes?

A: A seal.

Q: How many snails does it take to screw in a lightbulb?

A: Who knows? Nobody waits around long enough to find out.

Q: What kind of animals make the best detectives?

A: Investigators!

- -

Q: What does a soldier wear in the summer?

A: Tank tops.

Q: What kind of shoes make fun of you?

A: Mock-asins.

Q: What kind of clothes do houses wear?

A: Addresses.

Q: What did the conductor say to the misbehaving violin?

A: "You're in treble!"

Jane: Where did you get your backpack?

Kate: That's a purse-onal question!

- -

Q: What kind of dog uses a microscope?

A: A Labrador retriever.

Q: What do you call a sad cantaloupe?

A: Melon-choly.

Q: Where does a crocodile keep its milk?

A: In the refrige-gator.

Q: What do snowmen like on their cupcakes?

A: Frosting!

Q: Which kind of game makes you sneeze?

A: Domi-nose.

Q: When do sheepdogs cry?

A: When they're herding!

Q: What happened when the trees fell in love?

A: They got all sappy!

Bill: Did you like the sausage I cooked for you?

Joe: No, it was the wurst!

Q: How do you make a bug laugh?

A: Tickle it!

Q: **Why did the boy eat toaster waffles for breakfast, lunch, and dinner?**

A: His mom said he needed three square meals a day!

Q: **What do you call a camel with no humps?**

A: Humphrey.

Q: **What do you call a stick of dynamite that keeps coming back to you?**

A: A boomerang!

Q: **What did the stopwatch say to the clock?**

A: "Don't be alarmed!"

- -

Q: Why did the fawn put on a sweater?

A: Because it was buck naked!

Q: What do you give to a sick horse?

A: Cough stirrup.

Q: Where does a sick sailor go?

A: To the dock-tor.

Q: What do you get when you cross a toad and a pig?

A: A warthog.

Q: Why did the pig want to be a comedian?

A: He was a big ham!

Q: What did the pirate say on his 80th birthday?

A: "Aye, matey!" (I'm 80)

Q: What do horses do when they fall in love?

A: They get mare-ied!

Q: How do you fix a squashed tomato?

A: With tomato paste.

Q: Why did the science teachers fall in love?

A: They had great chemistry.

Q: Why did the horse put her foal to bed?

A: It was pasture bedtime.

- -

Ken: Do you like to eat venison?

Jen: It's deer-licious!

Q: Why do cows have hooves instead of feet?

A: Because they lactose. (lack toes)

Q: What do cows like to play at sleepovers?

A: Truth or Dairy.

Q: Why can't you trust a deer?

A: They'll always pass the buck.

Joe: You stole my cucumber!

Jon: What's the big dill?

Q: What kind of exercise should you do after you eat fast food?

A: Burpees.

Q: How do pandas fight?

A: With their bear hands.

Q: What do you get when you cross a robot and a pirate?

A: ARRRR2-D2.

Q: What is a unicorn's favorite vegetable?

A: Horn on the cob.

38

- -

Q: What is a sheep's favorite fruit?

A: Baa-nanas.

Q: Why was the dentist mad at the schoolteacher?

A: She kept testing his patients.

Q: Where do fairies go to the bathroom?

A: In the glitter box.

Q: What do you get when you cross a fish and a camel?

A: A humpback whale.

Q: What do you get when you cross a skunk and an elephant?

A: A smelly-phant.

Q: How does a mouse open the door?

A: With a squeak-key.

Q: Where do you keep a skeleton?

A: In a rib cage.

Knock, knock.

Who's there?

Repeat.

Repeat who?

Who, who, who . . .

Q: How do you call an amoeba?

A: On a cell phone!

- -

Q: How do you spot an ice-cream cone from far away?

A: With a tele-scoop.

Q: Why do you have to keep an eye on your art teacher at all times?

A: Because they're crafty.

Knock, knock.

Who's there?

Justin.

Justin who?

You're Justin time for dinner.

Knock, knock.

Who's there?

Howard.

Howard who?

Howard you like to let me inside?

Knock, knock.

Who's there?

Beets.

Beets who?

It beets me!

Q: What kind of fruit is never alone?

A: Pears.

- -

Q: What does peanut butter wear to bed?

A: Jammies.

Knock, knock.

Who's there?

Cash.

Cash who?

No thanks, but do you have any almonds?

- -

Knock, knock.

Who's there?

Feta.

Feta who?

I'm feta up with these knock-knock jokes!

Q: What did the frog wear with her dress?

A: Open-toad shoes.

Q: Where did the whales go on their date?

A: To a dive-in movie.

Knock, knock.

Who's there?

Lego.

Lego who?

Lego of the doorknob so I can come in!

- -

Q: What happened when the rabbits got married?

A: They lived hoppily ever after.

Pete: Did you hear about the guy that invented knock-knock jokes?

Dave: No, what about him?

Pete: He just won the no-bell prize.

Q: Why did the banker quit his job?

A: He lost interest.

Knock, knock.

Who's there?

Minnow.

Minnow who?

Let minnow if you plan on letting me in!

Knock, knock.

Who's there?

Ada.

Ada who?

Ada lot of candy and now I feel sick.

Tim: Did you hear the joke about the roof?

Mark: No, what is it?

Tim: Never mind. It's over your head.

Q: What kind of nuts are always catching colds?

A: Cashews!

- -

Knock, knock.

Who's there?

Espresso.

Espresso who?

Can I espresso much I want to come inside?

Q: What do you get when you cross an owl with a magician?

A: Who-dini!

Q: Why did the pony ask for a glass of water?

A: He was a little horse.

Q: What do you call it when candy canes decide to get married?

A: An engage-mint.

Q: What do you get if you scare a tree?

A: Petrified wood!

Q: How do you get straight A's?

A: Use a ruler.

Teacher: Please use a pencil for this test.

Student: What's the point?

Q: How did the music teacher open her classroom door?

A: She used a piano key.

- -

Knock, knock.

Who's there?

Tibet.

Tibet who?

Early Tibet, early to rise.

Q: What do you get when you cross a rabbit and a beetle?

A: Bugs Bunny.

- -

Knock, knock.

Who's there?

Dishes.

Dishes who?

Dishes a funny knock-knock joke!

Q: What do sheep eat for breakfast?

A: Goat-meal.

Q: What happened when the banana married

the orange?

A: They lived apple-y ever after.

Q: What do you call a girl who's

always wrong?

A: Miss-informed.

- -

Knock, knock.

Who's there?

Walnut.

Walnut who?

I walnut leave until you open the door!

Q: Why did the can stop talking to the can opener?

A: Because he kept trying to pry.

Q: What did one egg say to the other egg?

A: "All's shell that ends shell."

Q: What did the digital clock say to his mother?

A: "Look, Mom, no hands!"

Knock, knock.

Who's there?

Handsome.

Handsome who?

Handsome food to me—I'm starving!

- -

Q: Why did the boy stop carving the stick?

A: He was a whittle tired.

Q: How does a farmer greet his cows?

A: With a milk shake.

Knock, knock.

Who's there?

Watson.

Watson who?

Watson the menu for dinner tonight?

Q: Why did the monsters run out of food at their party?

A: Because they all were a-goblin.

Q: What can you break without touching it?

A: A promise!

Q: **What has to break before you can use it?**

A: An egg!

Q: **What do monkeys eat for lunch?**

A: Gorilla cheese sandwiches.

Knock, knock.

Who's there?

Otter.

Otter who?

You otter let me in!

Anne: Are you sure you want another cat?

Jane: I'm paws-itive!

Q: **Why did the music note drop out of college?**

A: It couldn't pick a major.

Jim: I have a henway in my pocket!

Joe: What's a henway?

Jim: About four or five pounds.

Q: Why did the pig go into the kitchen?

A: It felt like bacon a cake.

Q: What do cats put in their iced tea?

A: Mice cubes.

- -

Knock, knock.

Who's there?

Donut.

Donut who?

Donut make sense to let me in?

Q: What do you call a shape that isn't there?

A: An octo-gone.

Q: Why don't Dalmatians like hide-and-seek?

A: They're always spotted.

Knock, knock.

Who's there?

P.

P who?

I don't smell that bad!

Knock, knock.

Who's there?

Bean.

Bean who?

It's bean fun telling knock-knock jokes!

Q: What do you call an army of babies?

A: An infantry.

Q: Why couldn't the skunk go shopping?

A: He didn't have a cent. (scent)

Q: Why is it hard to have fish for dinner?

A: Because they're such picky eaters.

Knock, knock.

Who's there?

Romaine.

Romaine who?

Romaine calm and let me in!

Q: Why did the tuba stay after school?

A: Because it needed a tooter. (tutor)

- - - - - - - - - - - - - - - - - - - -

Knock, knock.

Who's there?

Wheeze.

Wheeze who?

Wheeze going to tell a lot more knock-knock jokes!

Knock, knock.

Who's there?

Toad.

Toad who?

I toad you to let me in!

Knock, knock.

Who's there?

Pizza.

Pizza who?

You want a pizza me?!

Q: Where do pigs keep their dirty clothes?

A: In the hamper.

Q: What do you get if you're allergic to noodles?

A: Macaroni and sneeze.

Sue: I finally got my new alarm clock.

Sal: It's about time!

Q: What do golfers drink out of?

A: Tee-cups.

- -

Q: What do dogs do when they're scared?

A: They flea! (flee)

Q: What did the baker say to the bread?

A: "I knead you!"

Q: What did the baker give his wife

for Valentine's Day?

A: Candy and flours.

Q: What kind of bread has a bad attitude?

A: Sourdough.

Q: When is music sticky?

A: When it's on tape.

Hannah: Did you finish your panda costume

for Halloween?

Emily: Bearly!

Q: Where did the composer keep

his sheet music?

A: In a Bachs.

- -

Q: What happened to the noodle that went down the drain?

A: He pasta way.

Q: What language do ducks speak?

A: Portu-geese.

Knock, knock.

Who's there?

Iguana.

Iguana who?

Iguana come inside and tell more jokes!

Q: Why did the chef quit making spaghetti sauce?

A: He ran out of thyme!

- -

Q: What did the mommy elephant say to her baby?

A: "I love you a ton!"

Knock, knock.

Who's there?

Sid.

Sid who?

Sid down and I'll tell you some jokes!

Knock, knock.

Who's there?

Twister.

Twister who?

Twister key and unlock the door!

Q: Why was the cucumber so upset?

A: Because it was in a pickle.

Q: Why did the teacher take away the kids' soda?

A: They failed their pop quiz.

Q: Why do monkeys like bananas?

A: They find them a-peeling.

Q: Where do cows go for lunch?

A: The calf-eteria.

Q: How do alligators give people a call?

A: They croco-dial the phone.

Q: How did the lizard remodel its bathroom?

A: With reptiles.

Knock, knock.

Who's there?

Moth.

Moth who?

Moth thumb got slammed in the door!

- -

Knock, knock.

Who's there?

Aspen.

Aspen who?

Aspen wanting to tell more knock-knock jokes!

Tom: I don't want to finish my steak!

Mom: Quit beefing about it!

Knock, knock.

Who's there?

Annie.

Annie who?

Annie way you can open this door and let me in?

Q: Why did the baker go to the bank?

A: Because he kneaded more dough!

Joe: Do you like your new beard?

Phil: It's growing on me.

Q: How many animals did Moses take on the ark?

A: None, it was Noah's ark!

- -

Knock, knock.

Who's there?

Mustache.

Mustache who?

I mustache if you're going to let me in!

Q: What muscle never says "hello"?

A: A bye-cep!

Q: What kind of fruit is hard to chew?

A: A pome-granite!

Q: How does an angel light a candle?

A: With a match made in heaven.

Q: Where does spaghetti like to dance?

A: At the meatball.

Q: Why was the man running in circles around his bed?

A: He was trying to catch up on his sleep.

Q: What is a wasp's favorite hairstyle?

A: A beehive.

Q: What kind of bee likes sushi?

A: A wasa-bee. (wasabi)

Q: What kind of dessert do you eat in the bathtub?

A: Sponge cake.

Knock, knock.

Who's there?

Radio.

Radio who?

Radio not, here I come!

Knock, knock.

Who's there?

Turnip.

Turnip who?

Turnip the heat—it's freezing!

Q: Why did the panda join the choir?

A: He was a bear-itone!

- -

Knock, knock.

Who's there?

Macon.

Macon who?

I'm Macon some eggs and bacon.

    You want some?

Knock, knock.

Who's there?

Shell.

Shell who?

Shell be coming around the mountain when

    she comes.

Q: When is butter contagious?

A: When it's spreading!

Knock, knock.

Who's there?

Hank.

Hank who?

Hank you for answering the door!

Knock, knock.

Who's there?

Mason.

Mason who?

**It's pretty a-Mason that I'm still knocking after
   all these years!**

Knock, knock.

Who's there?

Token.

Token who?

I'm token to you. Let me in!

Q: What kind of word can't wait to be used?

A: A now-n. (noun)

Q: Why did the skeleton's mom tell him to eat more?

A: Because he was boney.

Q: What does Miss America drink?

A: Beau-tea!

Q: What do you call a locksmith that's in a
bad mood?

A: Crank-key!

Knock, knock.

Who's there?

Izzy.

Izzy who?

Izzy going to open the door or not?

Knock, knock.

Who's there?

Butter.

Butter who?

You butter open up or else!

Knock, knock.

Who's there?

You.

You who?

I'm the one knocking, what do you want?!

Q: What do you call a really smart bug?

A: Brilli-ant!

Knock, knock.

Who's there?

Nose.

Nose who?

I nose you want to open the door, so go ahead.

Knock, knock.

Who's there?

Wool.

Wool who?

Wool you make me a sandwich?

Knock, knock.

Who's there?

Lena.

Lena who?

Lena little closer—I want to tell you a secret.

Q: Why is the teacher in charge everywhere she goes?

A: She controls all the rulers.

Q: What do you call a cobra without clothes?

A: S-naked.

Knock, knock.

Who's there?

Honeybee.

Honeybee who?

Honeybee a dear and open the door.

- -

Knock, knock.

Who's there?

Peeka.

Peeka who?

No, it's peekaboo!

Knock, knock.

Who's there?

Colin.

Colin who?

Colin it a day! It's time to go.

Q: What is a chimpanzee's favorite drink?

A: Ape-le juice.

Q: Why couldn't the Little Pig run away from the Big Bad Wolf?

A: He pulled a hamstring!

- -

Q: What is a bird's favorite subject in school?

A: Owl-gebra.

Q: Why was the bacon laughing so hard?

A: Because the egg cracked a yoke!

Knock, knock.

Who's there?

Waddle.

Waddle who?

Waddle I do if you don't open the door?

Knock, knock.

Who's there?

Hugo.

Hugo who?

Hugo and tell mom I'm at

   the door right now!

- -

Q: Why does everybody like baby cows?

A: They're adora-bull!

Knock, knock.

Who's there?

Gnat.

Gnat who?

It's gnat cool that I've been knocking all this
time and you've still not opened the door!

Knock, knock.

Who's there?

Howl.

Howl who?

Howl I get in if you don't open the door?

Q: Why did the gorilla stop eating bananas?

A: He lost his ape-tite.

Q: Why was the oak tree so proud of

his heritage?

A: Because his roots ran deep.

- -

Knock, knock.

Who's there?

Honeycomb.

Honeycomb who?

Honeycomb your hair!

Q: **What did the pig do when he wrote a book?**

A: He used a pen name.

Q: **What kind of flowers like to sing?**

A: Pe-tune-ias.

Q: **Why did the violin go to the gym?**

A: So it could stay as fit as a fiddle.

Q: **What does a baby ghost wear?**

A: Bootees.

Joe: Can you believe my dog caught a thousand sticks?

Jim: No, that sounds too far-fetched.

Q: How do you wash your stockings?

A: With a panty hose.

Q: Why did the vampire join the army?

A: So it could see combat!

Larry: I dreamed about a billboard.

Lucy: I think it's a sign!

Q: What do you get when paper towels fall asleep?

A: Napkins!

Q: What did the nurse say to the doctor?

A: "ICU!"

Q: How do you get your mom to make you some toast?

A: Just butter her up!

Knock, knock.

Who's there?

Casino.

Casino who?

Casino reason why you won't let me in.

- -

Q: How do you buy a tropical fish?

A: With ane-money!

Q: Where should a wildcat sleep?

A: Behind a chain lynx fence!

Q: Why did the ape ask for lemons?

A: So it could be orangu-tangy!

Knock, knock.

Who's there?

Toucan.

Toucan who?

Toucan play at this game!

- -

Knock, knock.

Who's there?

Alpaca.

Alpaca who?

Alpaca sandwich in my lunch box!

Q: How do you feel when a giant lizard steps on your toe?

A: Dino-sore!

Q: What's the funniest fish?

A: A piranha-ha-ha!

- -

Q: What kind of bird lives in a mansion?

A: An ostrich!

Q: What was Beethoven's favorite vegetable?

A: Bach-choy!

Q: What do you get when you cross vegetables and animals?

A: Zoo-chini!

Q: What do you call a book with sparkles?

A: Glitter-ature!

Q: What do you call a bunch of cows that live together?

A: A com-MOO-nity.

Q: Where can you read about coffee cups?

A: In a mug-azine!

Q: Where can you read about insomnia?

A: In a snooze-paper.

Q: Who says bad words at the store?

A: A cuss-tomer.

Q: How do you pay for the truth?

A: With a reality check.

Q: How do you feel when your shirt is wrinkled?

A: Depressed!

Q: How does a whale pay for its lunch?

A: With curren-sea.

Q: How does the sun say hello?

A: With a heat wave!

Q: Why did the skunk have to stand in the corner?

A: It was a little stinker!

Valerie: Do you feel better about yesterday?

Malorie: Yes, I'm past tense!

Q: What do you call soap wearing a tuxedo?

A: A detergent!

Lou: What happened to all your furniture?

Sue: I gave it to chair-ity.

Ben: My pants almost fell down!

Ken: That was a clothes call!

Q: When is a nurse an artist?

A: When they're drawing blood.

Mary: How do you feel about your braces?

Molly: En-tooth-iastic!

Q: Why did the pirate share his secret treasure?

A: He wanted to get it off his chest.

Q: When must you open the door?

A: When you're obligated.

- -

Q: Why did the diplomat become a brain surgeon?

A: He wanted peace of mind.

Q: How does a witch doctor stay in shape?

A: They hex-ercise!

Q: Why didn't the mice make cookies on Christmas Eve?

A: Because not a creature was stirring.

Knock, knock.

Who's there?

Design.

Design who?

Design says you're open, so let me in!

Q: How do you clean a pumpkin?

A: In a squashing machine.

Bella: You should write a book!

Stella: What a novel idea!

Q: What do you call it when you pass out the cards?

A: Ideal.

Q: What's the best time to get married?

A: On a Wednesday!

Q: What did one beekeeper say to the other?

A: "Mind your own buzz-iness!"

Q: What do you call a cow doing yoga?

A: Flexi-bull!

Q: What do bunnies like to play on the playground?

A: Hopscotch and jump rope!

Q: What do you call the selfie championships?

A: Olympics.

Q: Why did the boxer punch his oatmeal?

A: He was making his break-fist.

Q: Why did the meteorologist go home?

A: He was feeling under the weather.

Q: How is a professor like a thermometer?

A: They both have degrees.

**Q: Why did the tooth fairy fall in love with
the sandman?**

A: She thought he was dreamy.

Q: What kind of bugs work at the bank?

A: Fine-ants.

- -

Q: Where do you mail your clothes?

A: To your home address.

Q: Why don't dogs go to school?

A: They don't like arithme-tick.

Q: What's the funniest time of day?

A: The laughter-noon!

Q: What do you call a baby potato?

A: A tater tot!

Q: What do you call a zombie elephant?

A: Gro-tusk!

Q: What do you call a snowman that makes coffee?

A: A brrrr-ista.

Q: How does an artist cross the river?

A: He uses a drawbridge.

Q: What do beavers eat for breakfast?

A: Pas-trees.

Q: When is the storm coming?

A: Monsoon.

Q: What do you get when you cross a goldfish and a cupcake?

A: Muffins.

Q: Who takes care of a butterfly?

A: Its mother.

Knock, knock.

Who's there?

Jester.

Jester who?

Your jester one to open the door for me!

- -

Knock, knock.

Who's there?

Hebrews.

Hebrews who?

Hebrews coffee every morning!

Knock, knock.

Who's there?

Howell.

Howell who?

Howell I get in if you don't open the door?

Q: What does a rabbit keep forever?

A: Its family hare-looms.

Diner: This soup is too bland!

Chef: That's in-salt-ing!

- -

Q: **Why did the little boy have so many vegetables?**

A: He was a kinder-gardener!

Knock, knock.

Who's there?

Whitney.

Whitney who?

I can't Whitney longer for you to open this door!

Q: **What happened when the anchorman broke his leg?**

A: He got a newscast.

Q: **What kind of bird wins the lottery?**

A: A lucky duck!

- -

Q: What do you get when everybody comes to the ball?

A: Perfect attendance.

Q: Why did the baker go to the square dance?

A: It wanted to dough-si-dough.

Q: When is a wig expensive?

A: When you have toupée.

Q: What do you call a beautiful zombie?

A: Drop-dead gorgeous.

Q: How does an artist get clean?

A: He draws a bath.

Q: **How did the mop beat the broom in a race?**

A: It left the broom in the dust.

Q: **What happens if you get lost in the bathroom?**

A: You don't know where to go.

Q: **Who's in charge of the tooth fairy?**

A: The presi-dentist.

Q: **What does a wasp play at the park?**

A: Frisbee!

Q: **How do you feel after you steal all the blankets?**

A: You have a quilt-y conscience.

Q: What do bees like on their cupcakes?

A: Frosting!

Jeff: We're getting a brand-new scale.

Steph: I can't weight!

Q: What's a spider's favorite book?

A: Webster's Dictionary.

Q: Why should you go in the woods when you're tired?

A: For rest!

Q: How do you say hello to an ice-cream cone?

A: "Fro-yo!"

Q: What's a bird's favorite cookie?

A: Chocolate chirp!

Q: What do you give a kitten to help it grow?

A: Fur-tilizer.

Knock, knock.

Who's there?

Mighty.

Mighty who?

Mighty want to open the door soon?

- -

Knock, knock.

Who's there?

Wanda.

Wanda who?

Wanda come outside and play?

**Q: What do tornadoes use to keep
their balance?**

A: Hurricanes.

Knock, knock.

Who's there?

Emma.

Emma who?

**Emma about to climb
through the window!**

- -

Knock, knock.

Who's there?

Isabella.

Isabella who?

**Isabella going to work or do I have to
keep knocking?**

Knock, knock.

Who's there?

Ava.

Ava who?

Ava got a good feeling about this.

- -

Knock, knock.

Who's there?

Wyatt.

Wyatt who?

Wyatt taking you so long to answer the door?

Knock, knock.

Who's there?

Ruth.

Ruth who?

I have peanut butter stuck on the Ruth

    of my mouth!

- -

Knock, knock.

Who's there?

Owen.

Owen who?

You're Owen a lot of money lately!

Q: What did the zombie wear to bed?

A: A night-goon.

Knock, knock.

Who's there?

Maya.

Maya who?

Maya help you with your coat?

- -

Knock, knock.

Who's there?

Elise.

Elise who?

Elise I answer the door when people knock!

Q: What did the lemonade say to the iced tea?

A: "Hey, sweet tea." (sweetie)

Q: What do you call a lazy cow?

A: A meatloaf.

Knock, knock.

Who's there?

Quiche.

Quiche who?

Quiche me quick before I go!

- -

Q: What kind of monster tucks you in at night?

A: A mom-bie.

Q: Why did the kids go to the haunted house?

A: It was eerie-sistible.

Miley: Do you want to go fishing with me?

Alex: That's a fin-tastic idea!

Q: What kind of money is easy to burn?

A: In-cents. (incense)

- -

Knock, knock.

Who's there?

Yah.

Yah who?

What are you so excited about?

Knock, knock.

Who's there?

Lettuce.

Lettuce who?

Lettuce in and you'll find out!

Q: What's a pretzel's favorite game?

A: Twister.

Q: How do you make a milkshake?

A: Take it to a scary movie!

Knock, knock.

Who's there?

Luke.

Luke who?

Luke out the window and you will see.

Q: How did the banana get out of school?

A: It split!

Knock, knock.

Who's there?

Nana.

Nana who?

Nana your business!

- -

Knock, knock.

Who's there?

Joanna.

Joanna who?

Joanna come out and play?

Knock, knock.

Who's there?

Ken.

Ken who?

Ken you tell me a funny knock-knock joke?

Knock, knock.

Who's there?

Ice cream soda.

Ice cream soda who?

Ice cream soda you can hear me!

- -

Q: Why are babies good at math?

A: They have so much formula.

Q: How does the pirate put on his belt?

A: He swashbuckles it!

Q: Why was the nose sad?

A: Because everyone was picking on it.

Q: Why do fishermen have so many friends?

A: They're good at networking.

Q: What kind of bug is hard to understand?

A: A mumble-bee.

Q: Why did the school bus driver give the kids peanut butter sandwiches?

A: To go with the traffic jam.

- -

Knock, knock.

Who's there?

Tomatoes.

Tomatoes who?

I'm freezing from my head tomatoes!

Q: Why did the dog go to the groomer?

A: It was looking a little ruff around the edges.

Knock, knock.

Who's there?

Granite.

Granite who?

Don't take me for granite!

Q: What do you call a fireman who runs away?

A: A smoke defector!

Q: Why did the snail drink a big cup of coffee?

A: It was feeling sluggish.

Q: Who gave the mermaid a new nose?

A: The plastic sturgeon.

Q: Why didn't the golfer get anything done?

A: He was just puttering around.

Q: What kind of dog does Santa have?

A: A Saint Brrrr-nard.

Q: What is Frankenstein's favorite book?

A: *The Scarlet Letter.*

- -

Q: Why did the baker slice the bread?

A: He wanted to cut his carbs.

Q: What's a leprechaun's favorite kind of music?

A: Shamrock!

Q: What happens when your pile of bills gets too heavy?

A: You can't budget!

Q: What did the watch say to the clock?

A: "I don't want to wind up like you!"

Q: What do you get when you cross a flower and a pickle?

A: A daffo-dill.

Q: When does a comedian tell the truth?

A: When he's a stand-up guy.

Q: What do you sing when you're in love?

A: A valen-tune!

Q: Why can't you win a fight with a dictionary?

A: It always has the last word.

- -

Q: What's a boxer's favorite drink?

A: Punch!

Q: How does a chicken get over the flu?

A: It re-coop-erates.

Q: What do trees put on their salad?

A: Branch dressing.

Amy: Do you like your new hair color?

Ellie: Yes, I've dyed and gone to heaven!

George: I finally finished raking the yard.

James: That's a re-leaf!

Q: What's a plumber's favorite vegetable?

A: A leek!

- -

Q: What happens if you check out too many library books?

A: You'll overdue it!

Q: Why did the farmer have a needle and thread?

A: He wanted to reap what he sewed.

Q: Why did Little Miss Muffet have a scale?

A: So she could have her curds and weigh.

Q: Why is the sun smarter than the moon?

A: The moon just isn't as bright.

Knock, knock.

Who's there?

Geyser.

Geyser who?

Geyser just as good at telling jokes as girls.

- -

Q: Who's in charge of the lumberjacks?

A: The board of directors.

Q: Where do you keep a baby pig?

A: In a playpen.

Q: When should you do your math homework?

A: Calcu-later.

Dad: Do you like how I ironed your shirt?

Mom: Yes, I'm impressed!

Q: When do you quit doing laundry?

A: When you throw in the towel.

Q: When doesn't a cannon work anymore?

A: When it gets fired!

- -

Q: What do you get when you cross a trumpet and a watermelon?

A: A tootie fruity!

Q: What is an elephant's favorite dessert?

A: Hippopota-mousse.

Q: What's a farmer's favorite fairy tale?

A: "Beauty and the Beets."

Q: How do you carve a tombstone?

A: You engrave it.

Knock, knock.

Who's there?

Raymond.

Raymond who?

Raymond me to tell you another joke!

Q: What's a gorilla's favorite fruit?

A: Ape-ricots!

Q: How do you see a Dalmatian at night?

A: With a spotlight.

Knock, knock.

Who's there?

Window.

Window who?

Window I get to tell another joke?

Q: Why did the kids take the elevator?

A: Because it's not polite to stair.

Q: Why was the nose running?

A: So it wouldn't catch a cold.

Tongue twisters:

Green grass grows great.

Crushed nut clusters.

Ducks quack, chickens cluck.

My eyes spy pies.

Sheep sleep sweet.

Dump trucks drop rocks.

- -

Q: What kind of animal eats lots of cheese?

A: The Hippopota-mouse.

Q: What is a grandma's favorite kind of cookie?

A: Gram crackers.

Sam: Did you like your karate class?

Marcus: I got a real kick out of it!

Q: Why was the mustard embarrassed?

A: It saw the salad dressing.

Q: What kind of cat likes to swim?

A: A platy-puss.

Q: When do boxers dress up in tuxedos?

A: When they want to look so-fist-icated.

Q: What happened when the stray dog was captured?

A: It gained a pound.

Knock, knock.

Who's there?

Juicy.

Juicy who?

Juicy any reason I shouldn't tell another knock-knock joke?

Knock, knock.

Who's there?

Alex.

Alex who?

Alex plain the joke later!

Q: What kind of birds always get stuck in trees?

A: Vel-crows.

Knock, knock.

Who's there?

Police.

Police who?

Police tell me this isn't the end of the knock-knock jokes!